Pop-Up Gift Cards

ORIGAMIC ARCHITECTURE BY MSAHIRO CHATANI

ONDORI

Pop-Up Gift Cards

GIFT CARDS

GREETING CARDS (Beauty of Lines)

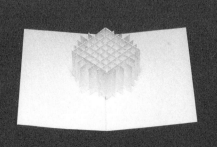

♠ MASAHIRO CHATANI
♦ KEIKO NAKAZAWA
♣ TAMAMI YAMAGUCHI
♥ ETUKO MOTOMURA

★ Published by ONDORISHA PUBLISHERS, LTD., 32 Nishigoken-cho, Shinjuku-ku, Tokyo 162, Japan
★ Sole Overseas Distributor: Japan Publications Trading CO., Ltd.
  P.O. Box 5030 Tokyo International, Tokyo, Japan
★ Distributed in the United States by Kodansha International/USA, Ltd.
  through Harper & Row, Publishers, Inc., 10 East 53rd Street, New York, New York 10022
  Australia by Bookwise International, 54 Crittenden Road, Findon, South Australia 5007, Australia

10 9 8 7 6 5 4 3 2 1

ISBN 0-87040-768-6
Printed in Japan

① Instructions on page 28.

② Instructions on page 29.

③ Instructions on page 23.

⑦ Instructions on page 32.

❾ ♡

❼ ◇

ETUKO MOTOMURA
6-1-3-711 OJIMA KOTO TOKYO

ORIGAMIC ARCHITECT
KEIKO NAKAZAWA
1-15-22-604 OKA ASAKA SAITAMA
TEL 0484-64-3066

ORIGAMIC ARCHITECT
KEIKO NAKAZAWA
1-15-22-604 OKA ASAKA SAITAMA
TEL 0484-64-3066

アトリエ・ブーケ
6-1-3-711 OHJIMA KOHTO TOKYO
TEL (03) 682-6909

アトリエ・ブーケ
6-1-3-711 OHJIMA KOHTO TOKYO
TEL (03) 682-6909

❽ ◇

❿ ◇

❻ ◇

11 ◇

12 ◇

14 ◇

13 ◇

15 ◇

16 ◇

19 ◇

20 ◇

17 ◇

18 ◇

21 ◇

 On Special Occasions

 **Flowers**

Various Shapes

49 ◇

50 ◇

51 ◇

49 Instructions on page 48.
50 Instructions on page 46.
51 Instructions on page 49.

52 ◇

54 ◇

53 ♠

ORIGAMIC ARCHITECT
MASAHIRO CHATANI

55 ◇

ORIGAMIC ARCHITECT
KEIKO NAKAZAWA

1-15-22-604 OKA ASAKA SAITAMA
TEL 0484-64-3066

52 Instructions on page 64.   54 Instructions on page 64.

53 Instructions on page 49.   55 Instructions on page 50.

Greeting Cards (Beauty of Lines)

Square Pillar 1. 2

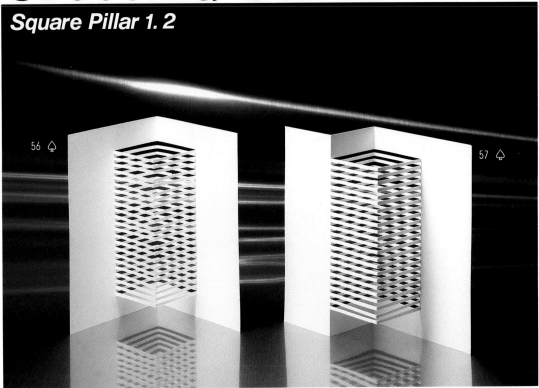

56 ♤

57 ♤

56 Instructions on page 34. 57 Sample

Wing 1. 2

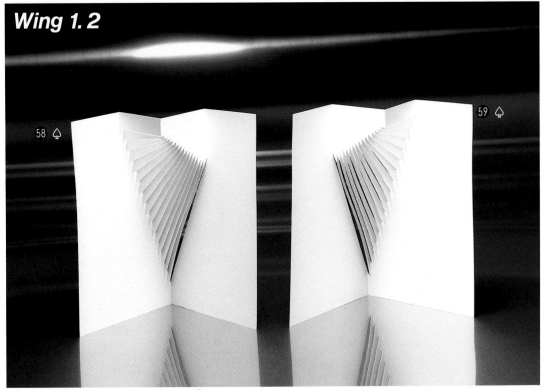

59 ♤

58 ♤

58 Instructions on page 35. 59 Sample

Cylinder

Prism

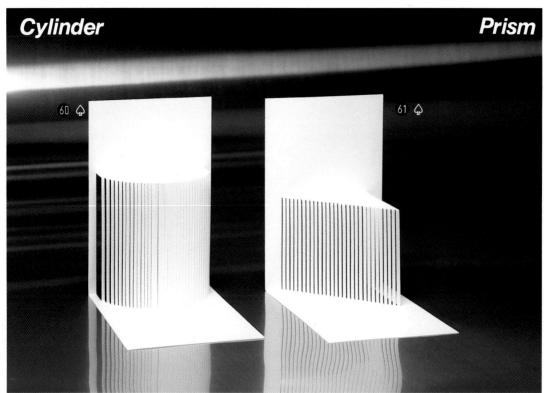

⑥⓪ Instructions on page 36. ⑥① Instructions on page 37.

Waves 1. 2

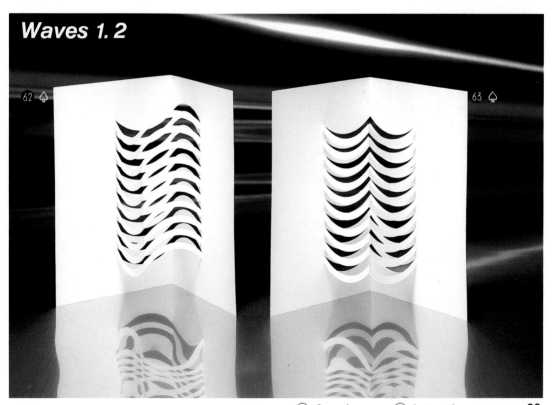

⑥② Sample ⑥③ Instructions on page 38.

Corridor 1. 2

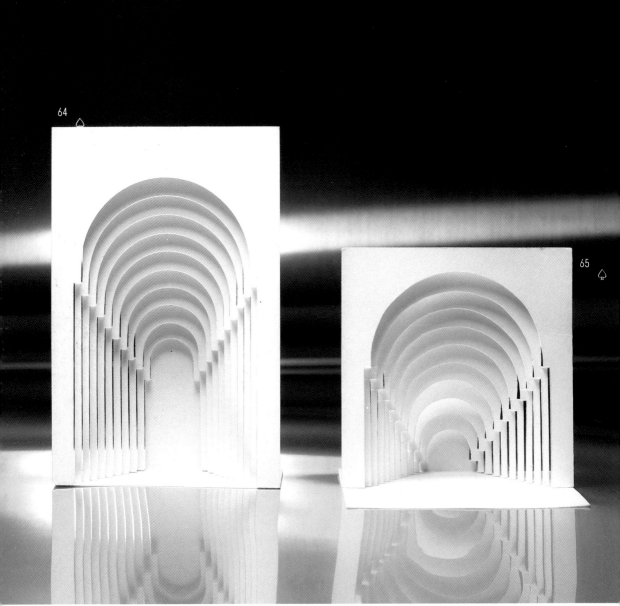

64 Instructions on page 39.
65 Instructions on page 40.

Mountain

Semicircle

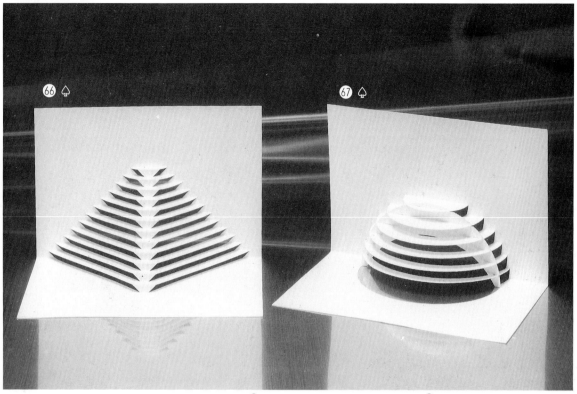

⑥⑥ Instructions on page 41. ⑥⑦ Instructions on page 42.

Seashells

Mysterious Stairs

⑥⑧ Instructions on page 43. ⑥⑨ Instructions on page 44.

Hyperbolic Paraboloid Curve ① ②

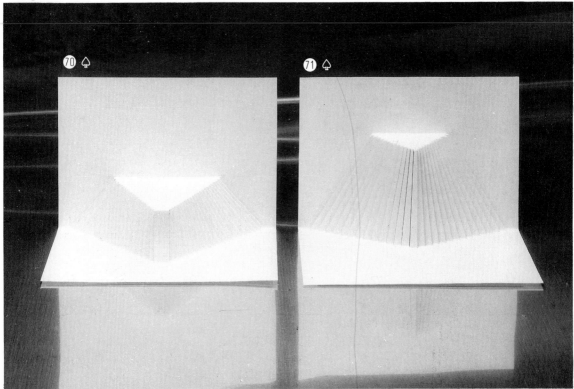

⑦ Sample　⑦ Sample

Hyperbolic Paraboloid Curve ③ ④

⑦ Instructions on page 45.　⑦ Sample

Basics in Origamic Architecture

❖ Materials and Tools

All the works shown in this book can be made with simple materials and tools. Your hands and head are the most important tools. However, the following materials and tools are required for the best results.

To make the 90° open type card:
1. Kent paper (To make a sample, use drawing paper or graph paper.)
2. Sketch pad
3. Gragh paper(1mm square)
4. Pencil(HB or H)
5. Eraser
6. Tracing paper
7. Clear plastic ruler
8. Steel ruler
9. Protractor
10. Cutting knife (Circle cutter works well for curves.)
11. Thick and thin stylus pen
12. Clear adhesive tape
13. Compasses
14. Pointed tweezers
15. All-purpose glue
16. Drafting tape

To make the new 180° open type card:
The following papers are required in addition to those above.
1. Kent paper for the base. Make sure of cutting into the indicated size.
2. Colored construction paper for decoration.

To make the ordinary 180° open type card:
In addition to those above for the 90° open type card, the following materials are required.
1. Kent paper for the base.
2. Kent paper for backing.
3. Japanese rice paper for reinforcement.
4. White cotton thread for attaching parts onto the base.

To make the Semi-dimensional card with shadow:
In addition to those above for the 90° open type card, colored construction paper for the backing is required to show the cut-out area in contrast.

About the paper:
All the cards except the greeting cards in this book are made of medium-weight, Kent paper 5.5cm by 9.0cm ($2\frac{1}{8}'' \times 3\frac{1}{2}''$) in size. The amount of paper required differs depending on the type of card and the layout of the pattern. Use two sheets of white Kent paper 5.5cm by 9cm or use white paper for the pattern and colored paper for the backing. Try to look for the most suitable paper for your design.

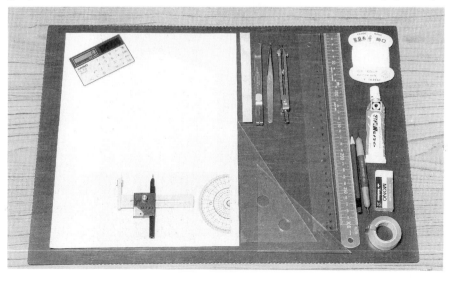

❧ Important Points in Making Pop-up Cards

1. To make the 90° open type card:

The 90° open type cards are made by cutting and folding as indicated. The main points in making the 90° open type cards are as follows:

How to cut the pattern:

Place a traced pattern on a sheet of Kent paper and transfer the pattern by perforating with a stylus pen. Using a cutting knife and a steel ruler, cut along the perforated lines. When cutting a sharp angel, cut each side toward the point. For curves, use a circle cutter or draw curves with a pencil and cut along pencil lines free hand. Make sure that cutting is done exactly along the lines.

How to cut a sharp angle

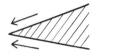 

How to crese:

A stylus pen is usually used for creasing. For a valley-fold line, score on the right side and for a mountain-fold line, score on the back. To make a neat fold line, cut at a depth of one-third of the thickness of paper on the right side. If you don't fold exactly, you may not obtain the desired shape. Begin folding from the corner of the longer fold lines using both hands. For the shorter fold lines, use the point of tweezers and fold exactly.

Backing:

All the 90° open type cards are made of a sheet of paper with pop-up design. However, if you use another sheet of Kent paper of the same color or drawing paper in contrasting color for the base, an interesting effect can be added to the card. Paper of the same size as the card is often used for the base, but if you glue two sheets of paper separetely onto each half of the card, you don't have to crease the center fold line and you can easily open the card. Use all-purpose glue for attaching the base. Carefully apply glue to the corners.

2. To make the 180° open type card:

It is sometimes defficult for a beginner to picture a completed three-dimensional design. However, I can say the 180° open type cards encompass all the most interesting features of pop-up designs. Please try making original cards following the instructions below.

Cut out parts:

The pattern for parts, unfolded shape and ground plan are shown for the 180° open type card. Cut the required number of parts as indicated.

Assemble the parts:

Assemble the parts following the photo. The points for assembling are given for each project, but think carefully before you start.

Attach cotton threads to the assembled parts:

The assembled parts are attached to the base at three or four places with cotton threads. Each thread is hooked onto concave part and tied or glued with a small piece of Japaneses rice paper. The places for attaching thread are indecated in the patterns. After assembling the parts, place them on the base and make sure of the exact points of attaching thread. Then, glue each thread with a small piece of Japanese rice paper.

Insert threads into holes and fix:

Insert the ends of thread (6—7cm)(2⅜″—2¾″) into the holes of the base, pull thread and fix onto the base temporarily with clear adhesive tape. Check whether the assembled parts pop up when the card is opened. If it works well, fix the end of each thread with glued Japanese rice paper. Trim off excess thread.

Attach another sheet of paper for backing:

Using another sheet of white Kent paper, back the base for reinforcement and for a neater finish. If you use two sheets of paper, the card can be opened easily. Glue a small piece of Kent paper onto each piece of Japanese rice paper as a final touch.

3. To make the new 180° open type card:

To make the ordinary 180° open type card, cut out all the parts, assemble and attach to the base with cotton thread and small pieces of Japanese rice paper. However, to make the new type, cut two halves of the base using a pattern and attach to the backing paper. A symmetrical shape is easier to make, but if carefully designed, you can make almost any kind of shape. For this type of card, prepare one sheet for backing and the other different size for the base and cut-out shape. Score along the fold line of the backing paper for easy opening.

4. To make the Semi-dimensional card with shadow:

This is a new type in this series. Once you have mastered the system, this is the easiest to make. The finished card, showing an interesting shape and its shadow in contrast, will surely appeal to many people.

....

Step-by-step Instructions for Making the 90° Open Type Card

㊸ **Block,** *shown on page 10.*

1. Prepare one sheet each of Kent paper 9cm by 11cm (3½″×4½″) and black construction paper in same size and the traced pattern.

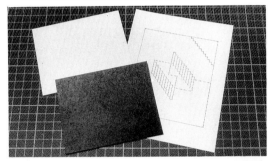

2. Place the traced pattern on Kent paper and fix them with Scoth tape. (If you print your name in advance, make sure whether it is placed properly.)

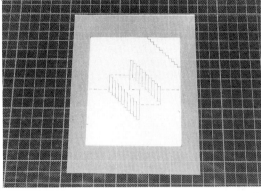

3. Perforate all corners and necessary points and score along the curves with a stylus pen.

4. Perforated pattern.

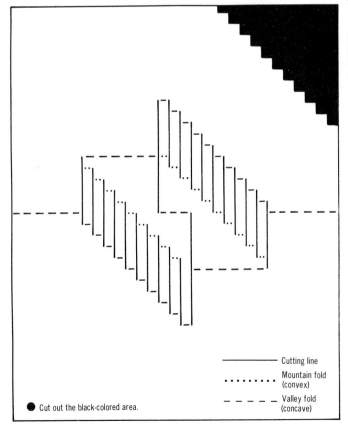

———— Cutting line

·········· Mountain fold (convex)

— — — — Valley fold (concave)

● Cut out the black-colored area.

21

5. Score along the mountain fold lines with a stylus pen first and then with a cutting knife cut half-way through the paper. Score along the valley fold lines on wrong side.

6. Cut along the cutting lines being careful not to cut beyond the lines nor to leave the uncut area (sea page 20 for cutting).

7. Start folding by pushing forward from the wrong side with your fingers.

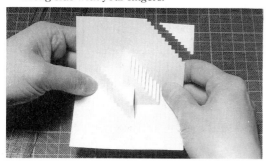

8. Score along the center fold line of the colored paper for backing.

9. Apply glue carefully.

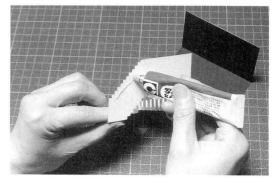

10. Finished card.

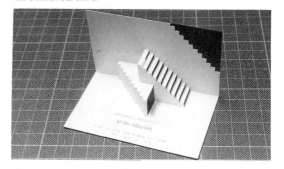

How to print

There are many ways of printing your name and address on the card. Of all the methods, I advise you to make use of a ready-made lettering set for a neater finish and easy handling. This also gives you various styles of letters from which you can choose the most suitable ones for your card. You may also use a typewriter or a word processor, but in this case you should print before you assemble the various parts into a card. It is a good idea to write with a pen, crayon, or watercolor paint. Neatly calligraphed cards will surely impress your friends.

Step-by-step Instructions for Making the 180° Open Type Card

③ Building, *shown on page 1.*

Prepare the following materials.

(a) 2 sheets of Kent paper for the parts, 10cm by 12cm (4″ × 4¾″).

(b) 2 sheets of Kent paper for the base, 5.5cm by 9cm (2⅛″ × 3½″).

(c) 2 sheets of Kent paper for the backing, 5.5cm by 9cm (2⅛″ × 3½″).

(d) Japanese rice paper for joint and reinforcement, 1cm by 9cm (⅜″ × 3½″).

(e) Cotton thread. (f) Patterns for the base.

1. Cut out all the necessary parts and check whether they match the traced pattern.

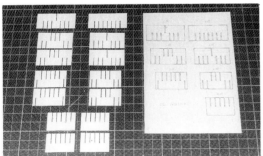

2. Starting at center, assemble the parts matching the joint.

3. Join the bottom part of each corner with Japanese rice paper to fix.

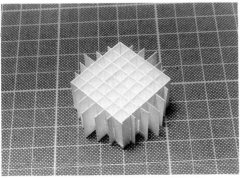

4. Attach thread to the marked place with glued Japanese rice paper using tweezers.

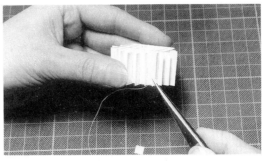

5. Place two sheets of Kent paper on the glued Japanese rice paper. Before the glue is completely dry, fold the base in half.

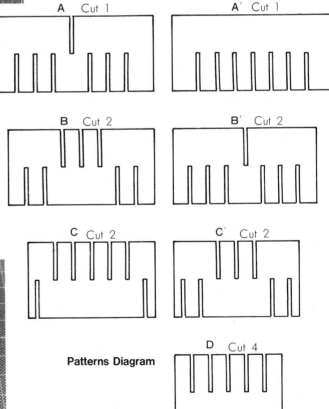

Patterns Diagram

A   Cut 1   A′   Cut 1

B   Cut 2   B′   Cut 2

C   Cut 2   C′   Cut 2

D   Cut 4

23

6. Make two holes in the base with a stylus pen.

7. Insert each end of thread into the hole using a tweezers.

8. Pull thread and fix it temporarily with drafting tape.

9. Check the shape of building, tension of thread and opening of the card. Reshape if necessary.

10. Remove the drafting tape and glue small pieces of Japanese rice paper to fix the thread. Glue Kent paper onto the underside of the base for backing.

11. Finished card.

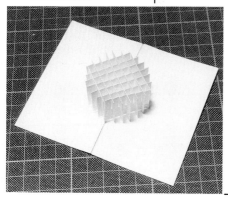

● Make hole at the dots and insert the end of cotton thread to fix the shape.

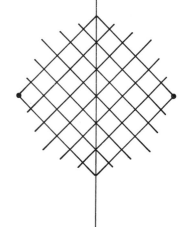

Step-by-step Instructions for Making the New 180° Open Type

㉔ **Butterfly,** *shown on page 6.*

1. The following papers are required for the new 180° open type card. (a) One sheet of White Kent paper for the base and shape, 9cm by 18cm (3 ½″×7″). (b) One sheet of Kent paper for backing, 9cm by 11cm (3 ½″×4 ½″). (c)Patterns for the base.

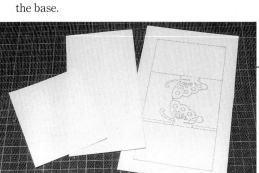

2. Place the traced patterns on Kent paper, fix them with Scotch tape, score along the patterns with a stylus pen and carefully cut along the cutting lines.

3. Cutting has been done.

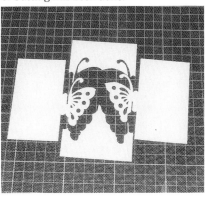

4. Score along the fold line (on the reverse side) and match the slits.

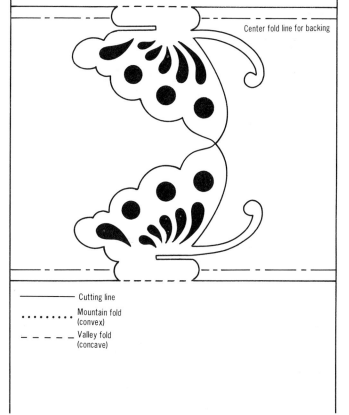

Center fold line for backing

———— Cutting line

· · · · · · · · Mountain fold (convex)

— — — Valley fold (concave)

5. Score along the center fold line of the backing paper. Apply glue onto the underside of each base and place on the backing paper.

6. Finished card.

Step-by-step Instructions for Making the Semi-dimensional Card with Shadow

㉘ Christmas Tree, *shown on page 8.*

(a) One sheet of White Kent paper for the base and shape, 5.5cm by 18cm (2 ⅛" ×7"). (b) 2 sheets of colored paper for backing, 5.5cm by 9cm (2 ⅛" ×3 ½"). (c) Patterns for the base.

1. Place the traced pattern on Kent paper and perforate along the pattern with a stylus pen. Remove the pattern and cut along the cutting line.

2. Cut out stars carefully. Set the cut-out stars aside for later use. Score along the center fold line.

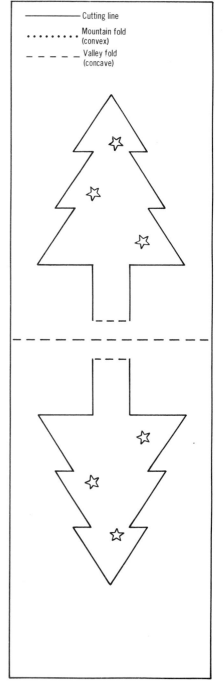

——————— Cutting line

· · · · · · · · Mountain fold (convex)

— — — — Valley fold (concave)

3. Fold the bottom of each tree toward the center and attach the top part of the trees together with glue.

4. Apply glue on the reverse side of the base and attach colored paper on the glued side.

5. Glue the stars in place.

6. Finished card.

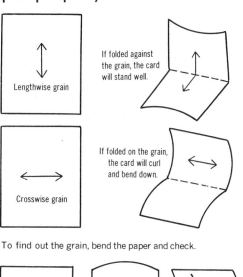

How to handle paper properly

Both Kent paper and colored construction paper are used for making pop-up cards in this book. The finished cards look neat when you handle them properly. Wood fibers have a tendency to run lengthwise in the process of making paper. Thus, most of paper has grain. When you make the 90° open type card, use the paper whose grain runs along the long side of the paper. If the paper is folded against the grain, it is at its best and stands well. On the other hand, if folded on the grain, it will curl and bend down. To find out the true grain, bend a sheet of paper of 10cm(4″) square. If the sheet is easily bent, it has a lengthwise grain. If not, it has a crosswise grain.

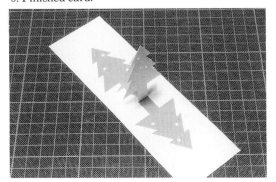

Lengthwise grain

Crosswise grain

If folded against the grain, the card will stand well.

If folded on the grain, the card will curl and bend down.

To find out the grain, bend the paper and check.

Lengthwise grain

Easy to bend   Hard to bend

Instructions and Actual-size Patterns

① **Flower,** *shown on page 1.*

2 sheets of Kent paper for parts, 10cm square.
2 sheets of Kent paper for the base, 5.5cm by 9cm.
2 sheets of Kent paper backing, 5.5cm by 9cm.
Japanese rice paper and sewing thread.

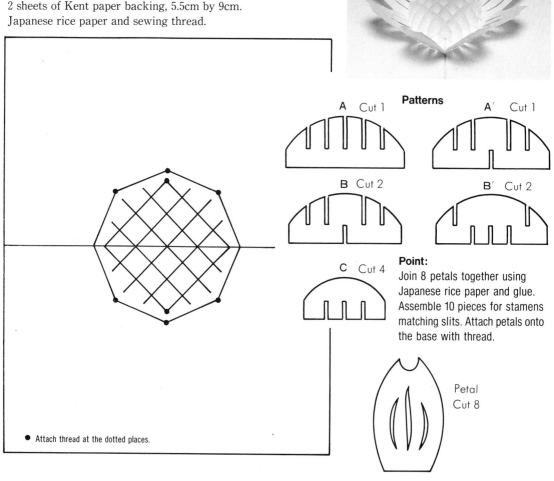

Patterns

A Cut 1

A′ Cut 1

B Cut 2

B′ Cut 2

C Cut 4

Point:
Join 8 petals together using
Japanese rice paper and glue.
Assemble 10 pieces for stamens
matching slits. Attach petals onto
the base with thread.

Petal
Cut 8

● Attach thread at the dotted places.

Visiting

In China, people used to exchange visiting cards on New Year's Day. For official use, people would fold a sheet of red paper into six, write their name on the front and put it into an envelope. A red strip of paper was used for private purposes. Korean people also had a similar custom. In Japan, visiting cards became common in the eighteenth century. The cards were made of heavy-weight hand-made paper with hand-written names. Some big stores distributed their cards to customers for New Year's greetings. Later, sending cards on New Year's Day placed a big bowl or box on a shelf in the front room for visitors to put their cards in. Today, exchanging business cards on first meeting has become the custom in the Japanese society. Even among students this cusom has become very popular recently. Many of them create their own original cards and compete in gift card contests. In the United

② **Cupola,** *shown on page 1.*

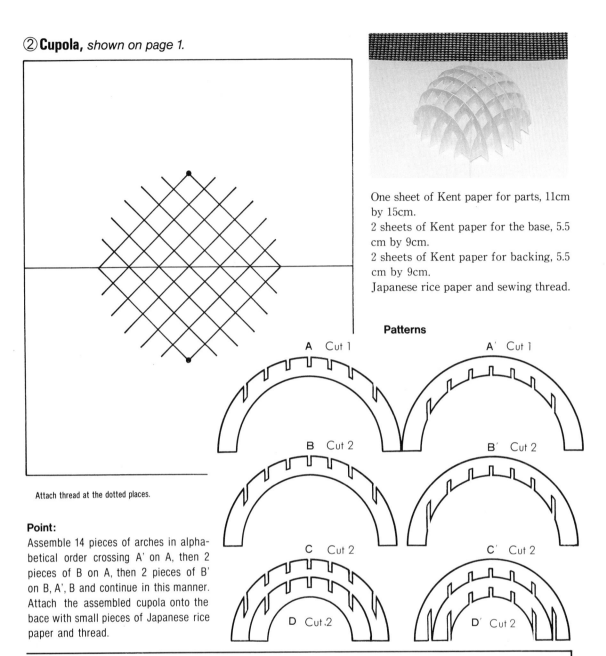

One sheet of Kent paper for parts, 11cm by 15cm.
2 sheets of Kent paper for the base, 5.5 cm by 9cm.
2 sheets of Kent paper for backing, 5.5 cm by 9cm.
Japanese rice paper and sewing thread.

Patterns

A   Cut 1

A'   Cut 1

B   Cut 2

B'   Cut 2

C   Cut 2

C'   Cut 2

D   Cut 2

D'   Cut 2

Attach thread at the dotted places.

Point:
Assemble 14 pieces of arches in alphabetical order crossing A' on A, then 2 pieces of B on A, then 2 pieces of B' on B, A', B and continue in this manner. Attach the assembled cupola onto the bace with small pieces of Japanese rice paper and thread.

Cards

Kingdom, tradesmen used Tradesmen's Cards or Trade Cards from the middle of the seventeenth century to the nineteenth century. Most of the cards had an illustration showing their business and the name and address of the tradesman. These cards were used as advertisements and as bills. The visiting cards and business cards have replaced the trade cards which showed many interesting aspects of business, fashions, buildings, tools of the time.

This book specializes in introducing unique pop-up visiting cards or message cards in handy size. Just imagine your friend's face when he or she has opened this unusual card made by you. Print your name and address using a typewriter, word processor or lettering set, or write them with a pen. We do hope you will enjoy making your original cards.

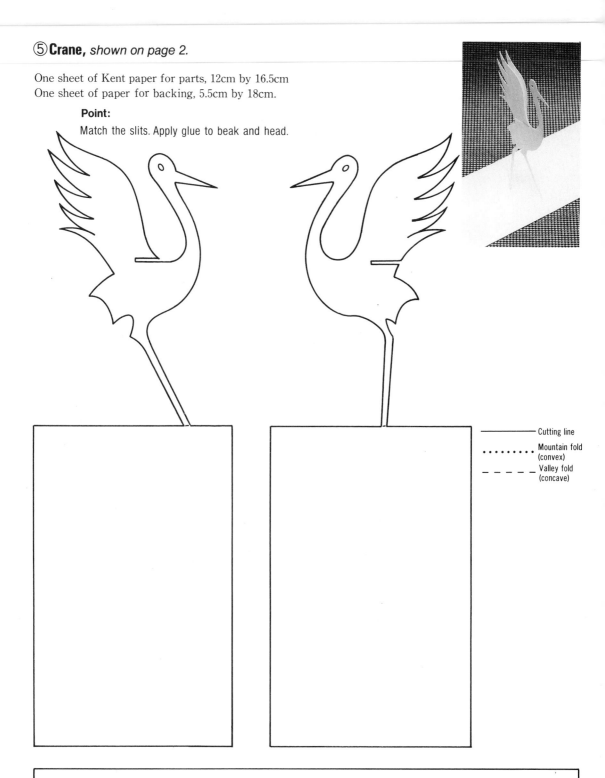

⑤ **Crane,** *shown on page 2.*

One sheet of Kent paper for parts, 12cm by 16.5cm
One sheet of paper for backing, 5.5cm by 18cm.

Point:

Match the slits. Apply glue to beak and head.

——————— Cutting line

• • • • • • • • Mountain fold (convex)

— — — — — Valley fold (concave)

Scoreing

When you see the word "scoring" in this book, cut one third of the thickness of the paper on the front side for the valley-fold lines and on the reverse side for the mountain-fold lines. This makes folding easy and neat.

⑮**Soccer,** *shown on page 4.*

One sheet of Kent paper for parts, 9cm by 16cm.
One sheet of paper for backing, 9cm by 11cm.
Apply glue to hand.

⑥**Egret,**

shown on page 3.

One sheet of Kent paper for parts, 5.5cm by 31cm.
One sheet of paper for backing, 5.5cm by 18cm.

Apply glue to head.

——————— Cutting line

· · · · · · · · Mountain fold (convex)

— — — — Valley fold (concave)

Center fold line for backing

Center fold line for backing

——————— Cutting line

· · · · · · · · Mountain fold (convex)

— — — — Valley fold (concave)

⑦ **Swan,** *shown on page 3.*

One sheet of Kent paper for parts, 9cm by 21cm.
One sheet of paper for backing, 9cm by 11cm.

Point:
Match the slits. Apply glue to beak and head.

㉚ **Christmas Tree,** *shown on page 8.*

2 sheets of Kent paper for parts, 5.5cm by 16cm.
One sheet of paper for backing, 5.5cm by 18cm.

Point:
You may cut two sheets of paper at one time.
Apply glue to star.

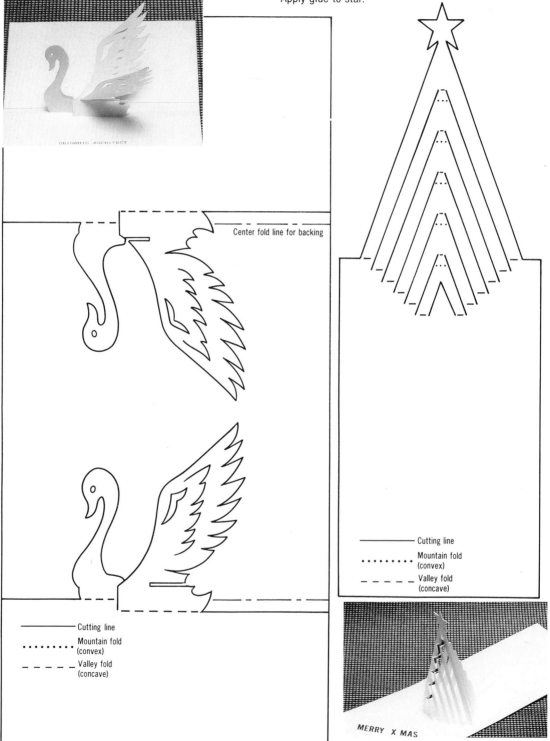

Center fold line for backing

Cutting line
Mountain fold
(convex)
Valley fold
(concave)

Cutting line
Mountain fold
(convex)
Valley fold
(concave)

MERRY X MAS

㉗ **Rabbit,** *shown on page 7.*

One sheet of Kent paper for parts, 9cm by 16cm.
One sheet of paper for backing, 9cm by 11cm.

Apply glue to muzzle and tail.

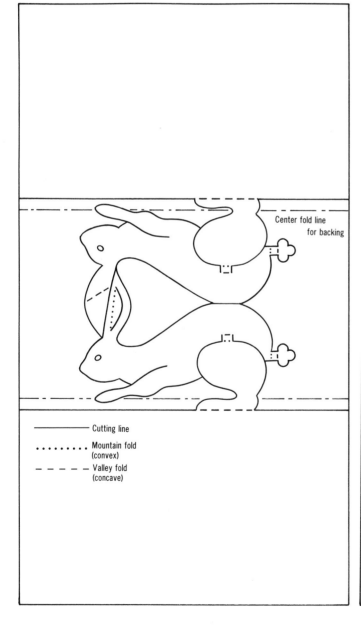

Center fold line
for backing

——————— Cutting line

• • • • • • • • Mountain fold
(convex)

– – – – – Valley fold
(concave)

⑪ **Skier,** *shown on page 4.*

One sheet of Kent paper for parts, 5.5cm by 28cm.
One sheet of paper for backing, 5.5cm by 18cm.

Apply glue to head.

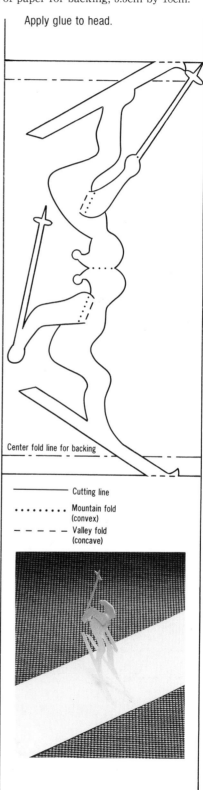

Center fold line for backing

——————— Cutting line

• • • • • • • • Mountain fold
(convex)

– – – – – Valley fold
(concave)

㉟ **Square Pillar,** *shown on page 14.*

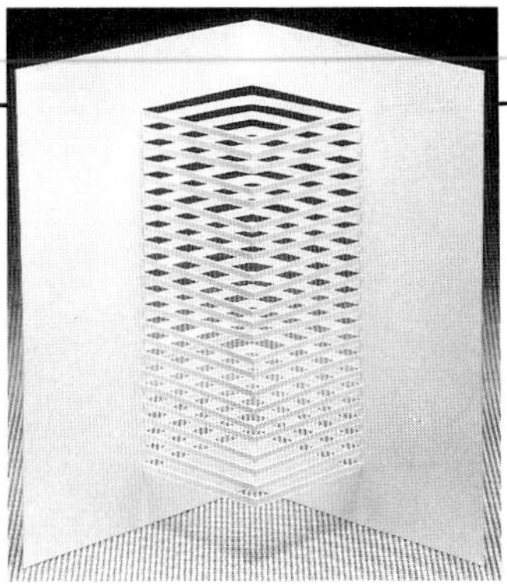

———— Cutting line

• • • • • • • • Mountain fold (convex)

— — — — Valley fold (concave)

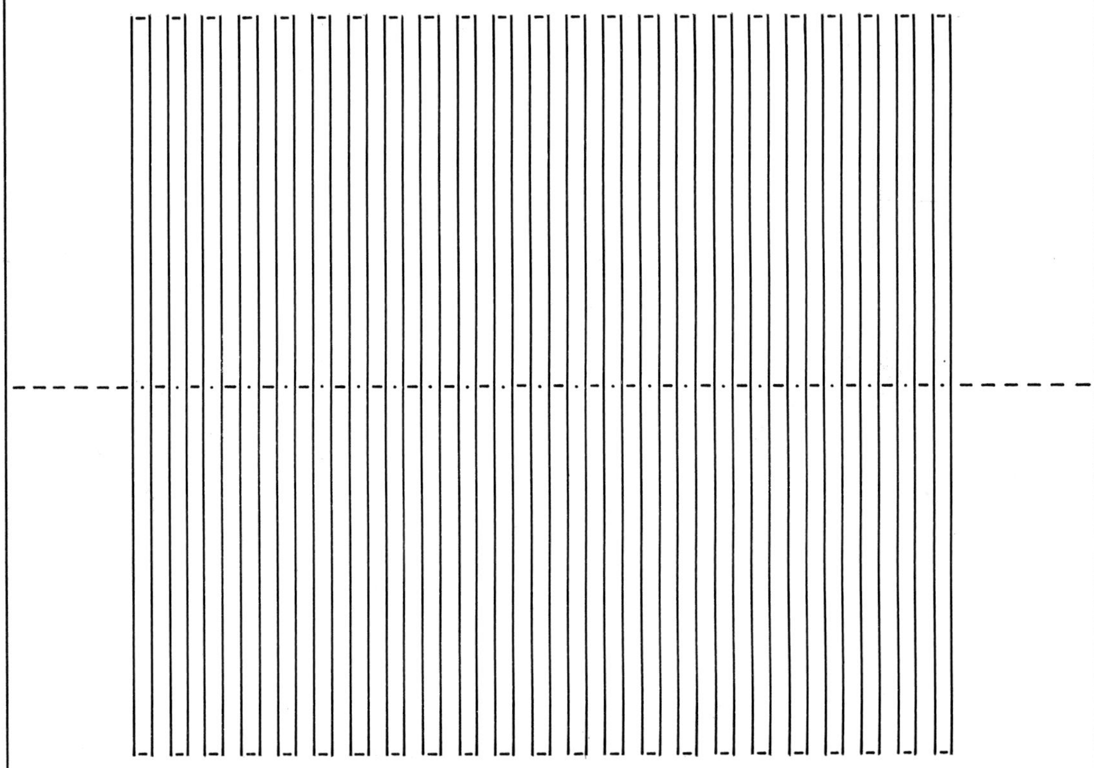

57 is a variation of 56. Fold one quarter of the base as shown. You can make many variations changing the valley-fold line to the mountain-fold line and vice versa.

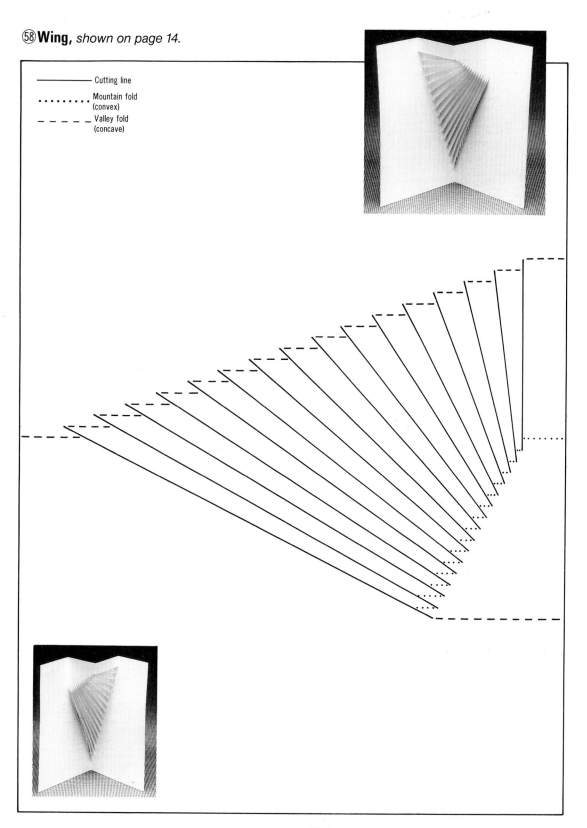

58 **Wing,** *shown on page 14.*

——————— Cutting line

• • • • • • • • Mountain fold (convex)

— — — — — Valley fold (concave)

59 is a reversed shape of 58. Mountain-fold line and valley-fold lines are same.

60 Cylinder,

shown on page 15.

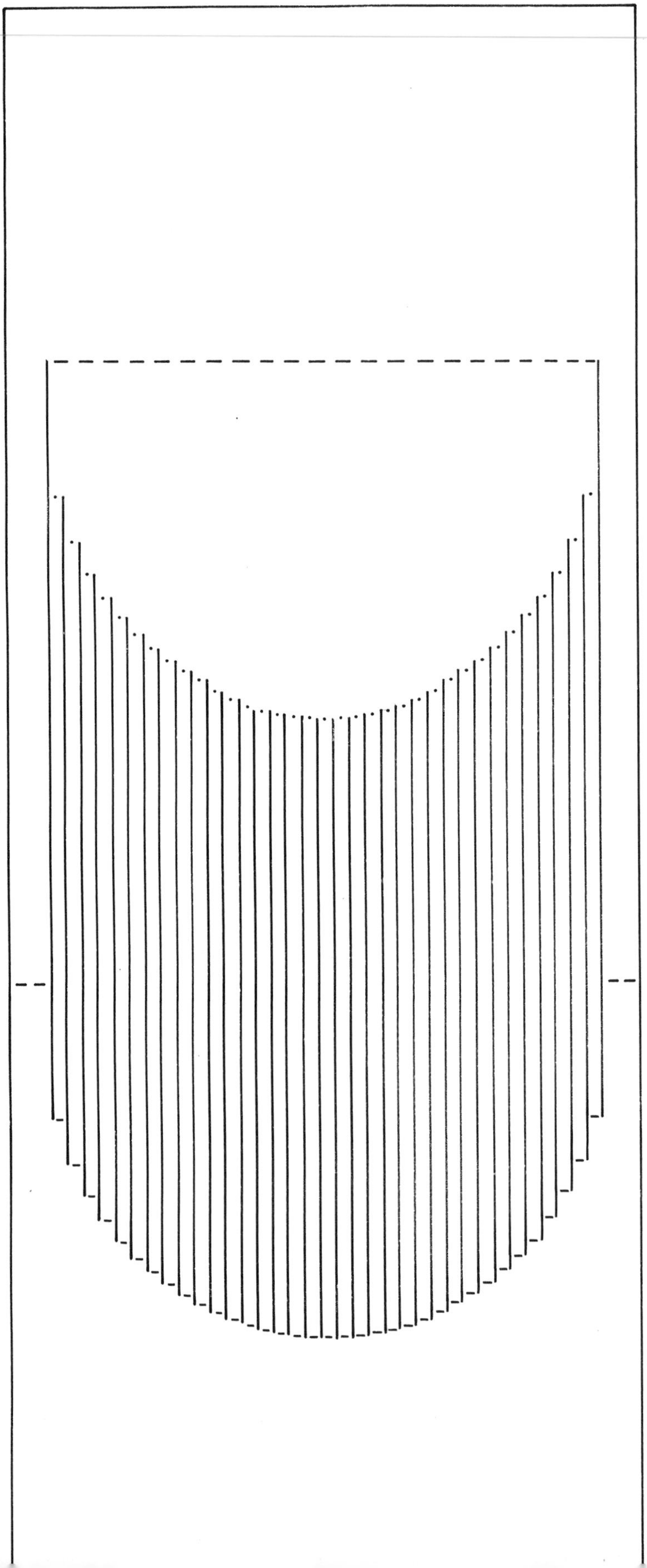

——————— Cutting line

•••••••• Mountain fold
(convex)

— — — — Valley fold
(concave)

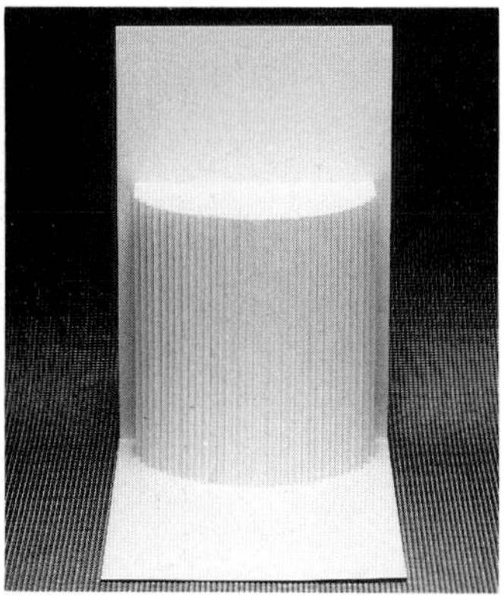

Cutting line

· · · · · · · Mountain fold
(convex)

— — — Valley fold
(concave)

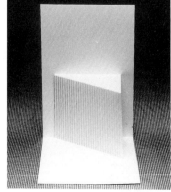

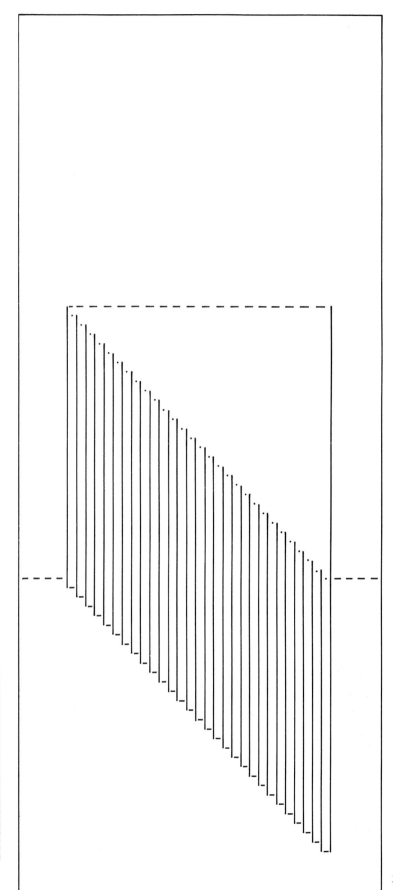

㉖ **Waves,** *shown on page 15.*

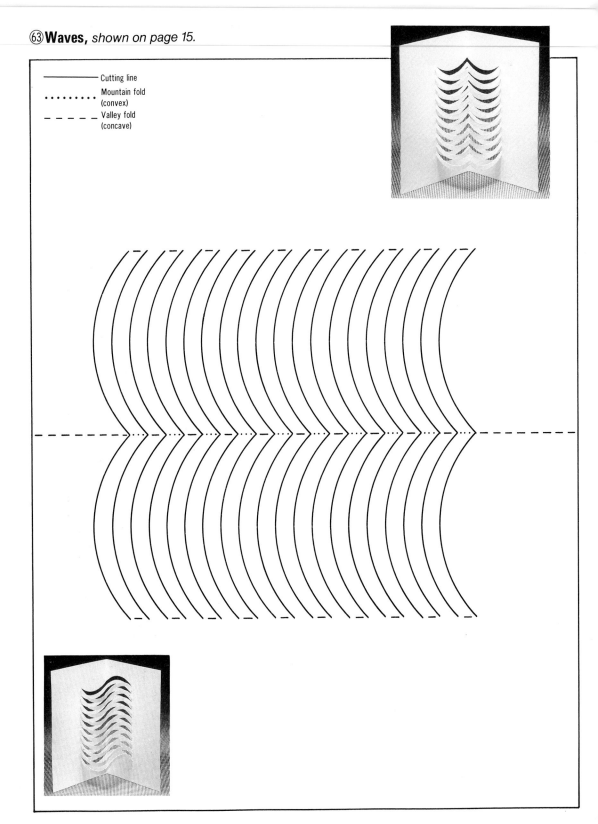

Cutting line

Mountain fold
(convex)

Valley fold
(concave)

62 is made by changing the direction of the waves of
left side. The finished shape looks quite different from 63.

�64 Corridor,

shown on page 16.

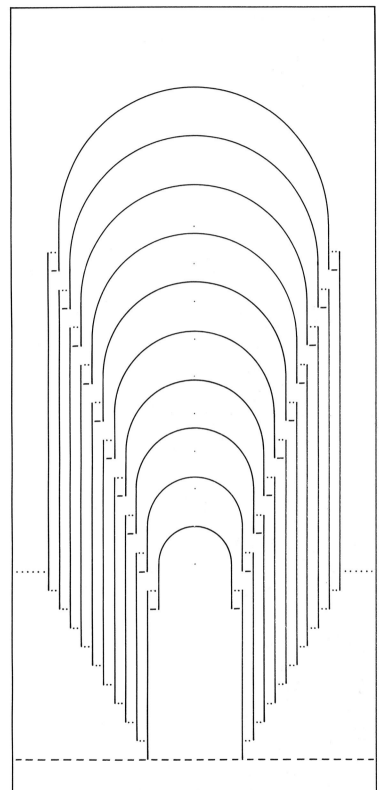

——— Cutting line

••••••••• Mountain fold
(convex)

— — — — Valley fold
(concave)

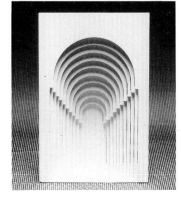

5
cm

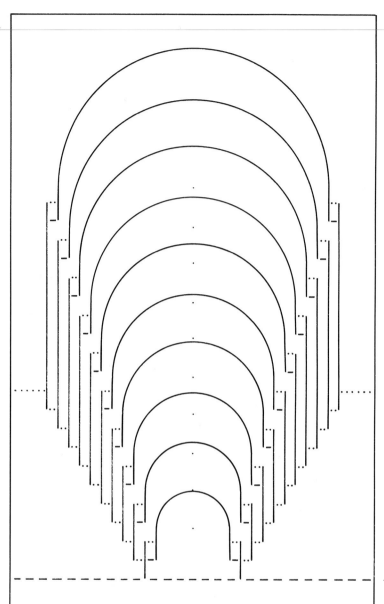

Cutting line
.... Mountain fold
(convex)
– – – – Valley fold
(concave)

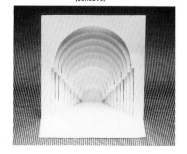

IO
cm

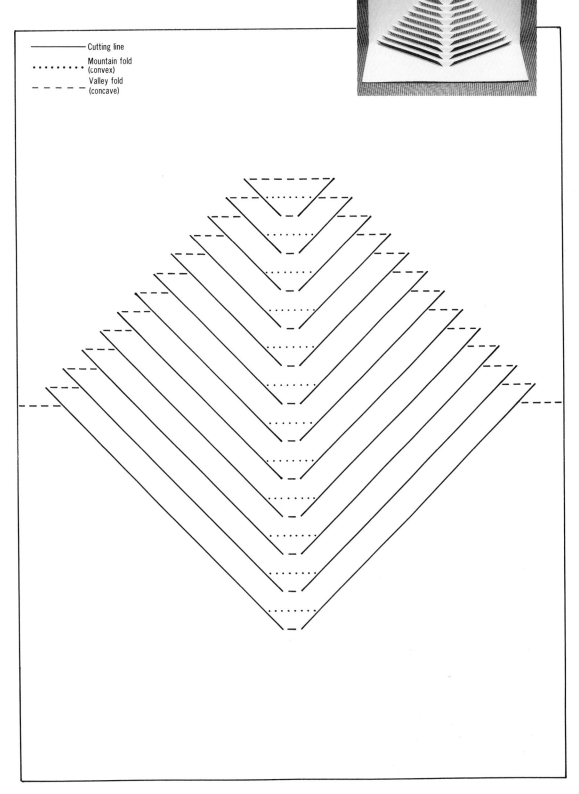

—————— Cutting line

• • • • • • • Mountain fold
(convex)

— — — — Valley fold
(concave)

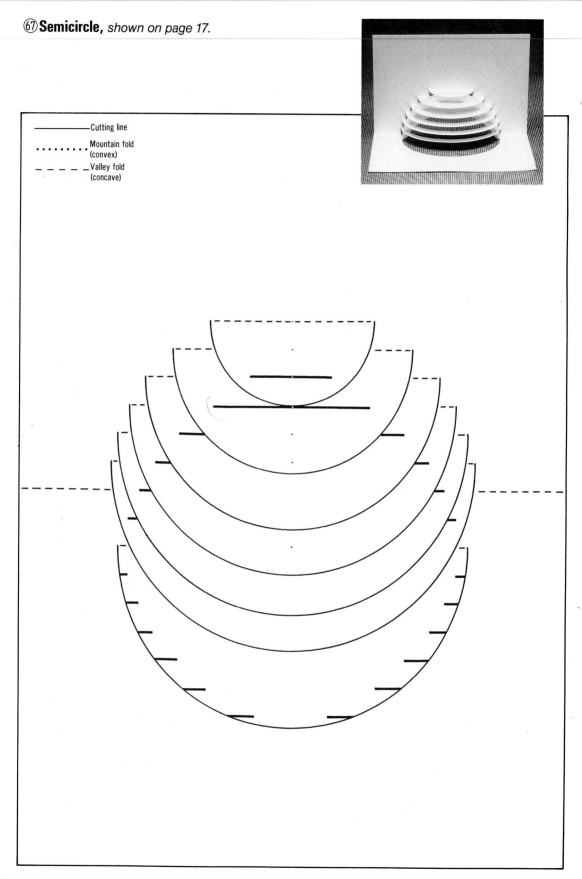

Cutting line

Mountain fold
(convex)

Valley fold
(concave)

⑱ Seashells, *shown on page 17.*

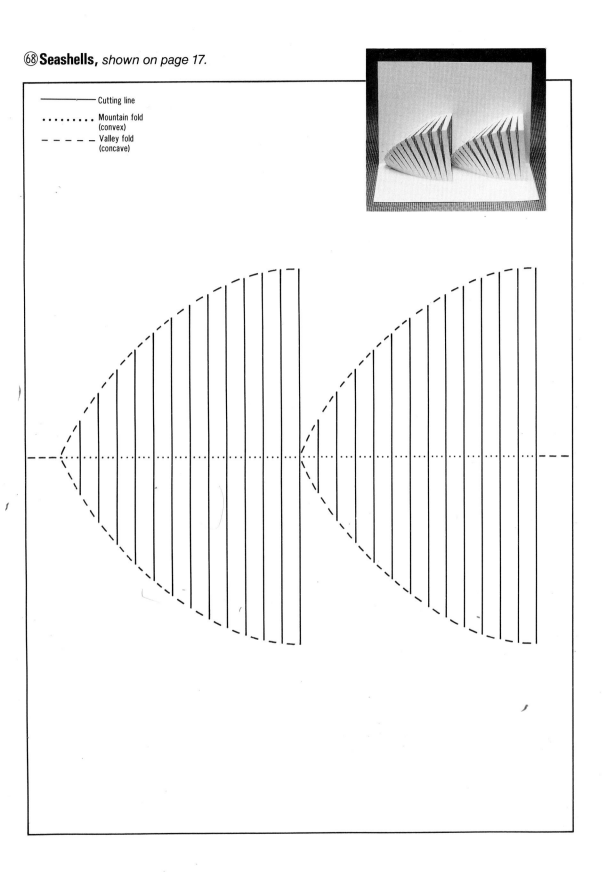

Cutting line

•••••••• Mountain fold
(convex)

— — — Valley fold
(concave)

㊉ **Mysterious Stairs,** *shown on page 17.*

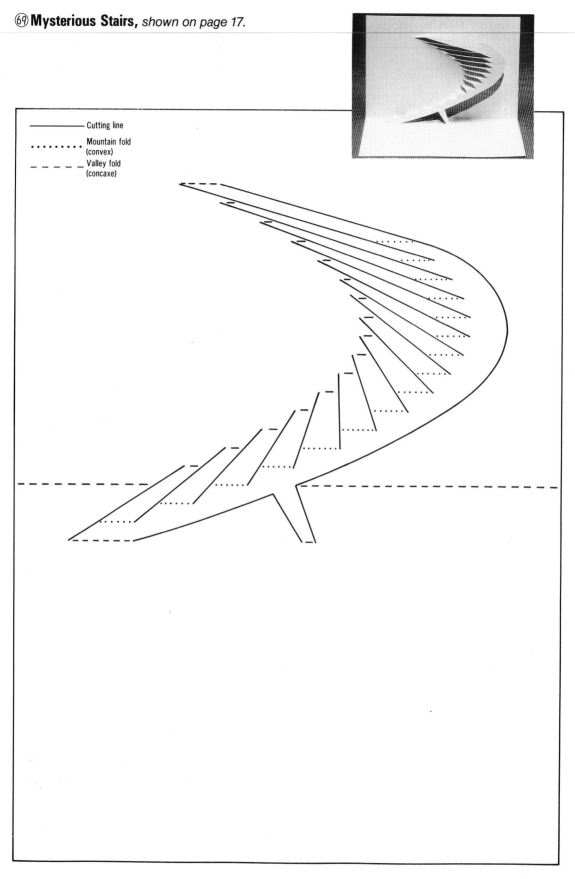

- ——————— Cutting line
- • • • • • • • • Mountain fold (convex)
- — — — — Valley fold (concaxe)

㊵Hyperbolic Paraboloid Curve,

shown on page 18, bottom left.

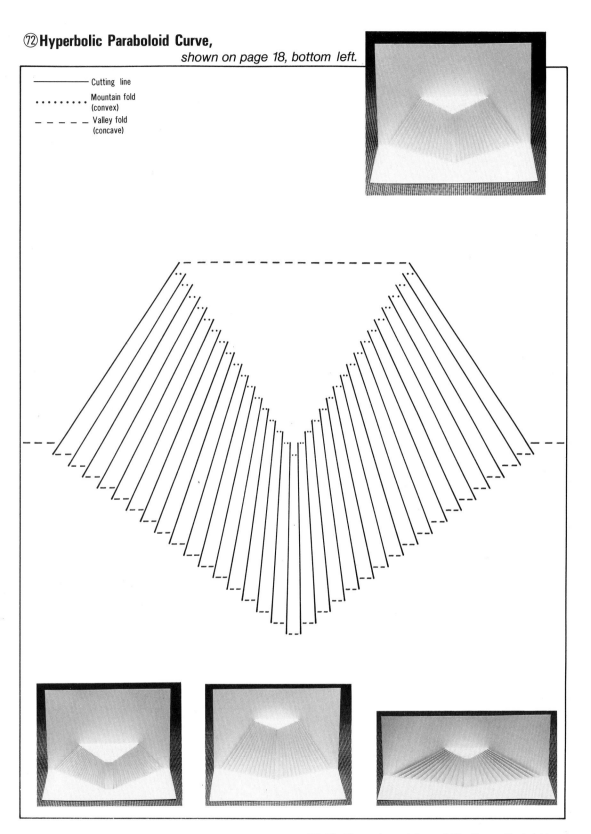

——————— Cutting line

• • • • • • • • Mountain fold
(convex)

— — — — — Valley fold
(concave)

70, 71, 73 are the variations of 72. Change the height and the width of the stand. The top triangle is the same.

This is a sample of the lettering. Capitals and small letters are shown for your reference. Make your name card using these letters or you may slant all the letters for a different look. Try to create your own original style.

——————— Cutting line

•••••••••• Mountain fold (convex)

– – – – – Valley fold (concave)

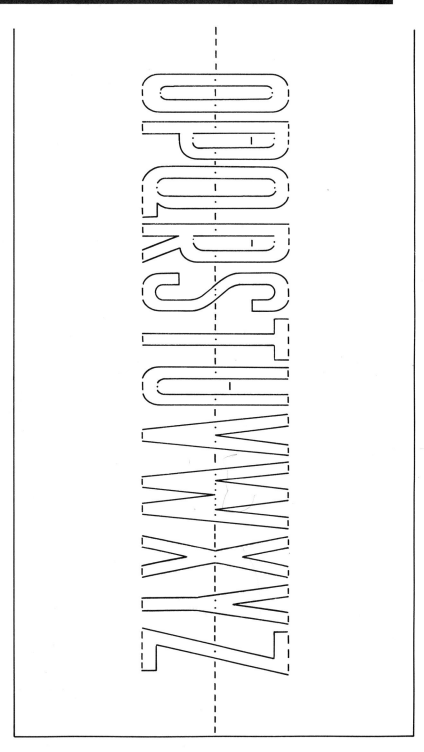

——————— Cutting line

• • • • • • • • • Mountain fold
(convex)

— — — — — Valley fold
(concave)

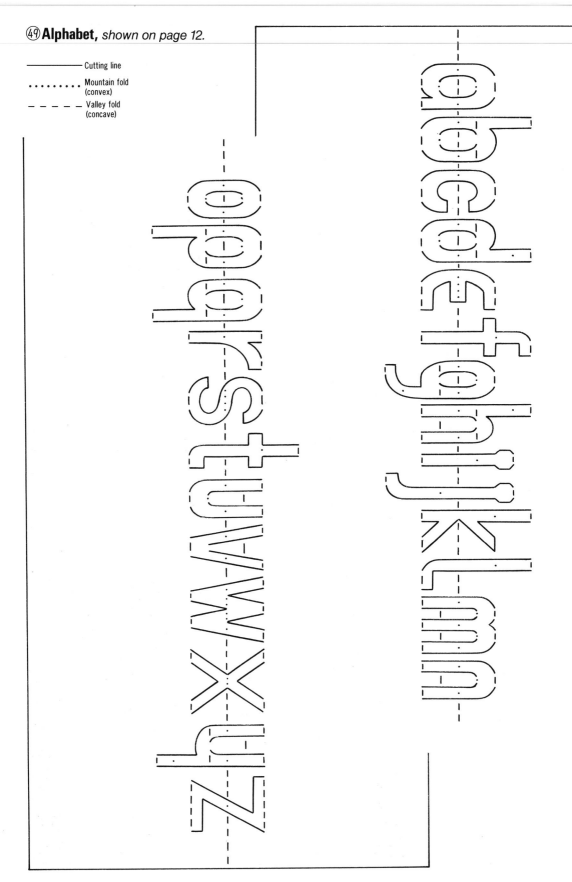

(53) **Name,** *shown on page 13.*

Cutting line

Mountain fold (convex)

Valley fold (concave)

(51) **Name,** *shown on page 12.*

Point:
Use colored paper for backing.

● Cut out black area.

Cutting line

Mountain fold (convex)

Valley fold (concave)

㉟ **Name,** *shown on page 13.*

Point:

Use colored paper for backing.

————— Cutting line

· · · · · · · · · Mountain fold
(convex)

— — — Valley fold
(concave)

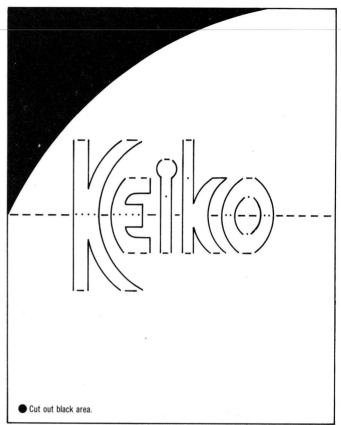

● Cut out black area.

㉝ **Flower Garden,** *shown on page 9.*

Point:

Use colored paper for backing.

————— Cutting line

· · · · · · · · · Mountain fold
(convex)

— — — Valley fold
(concave)

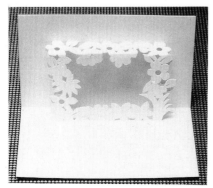

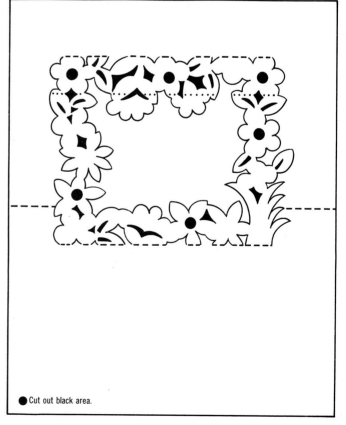

● Cut out black area.

45 **Egg,** *shown on page 11.*

Point:

Use colored paper for backing.

Apply glUe to top.

——————— Cutting line

• • • • • • • • • Mountain fold
(convex)

– – – – – Valley fold
(concave)

18 **Golfer,**

shown on page 5.

Apply glue to head
elbow and hand.

——————— Cutting line

• • • • • • • • • Mountain fold
(convex)

– – – – – Valley fold
(concave)

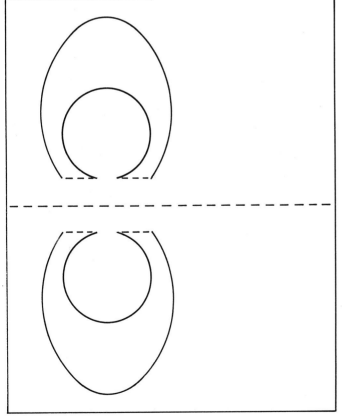

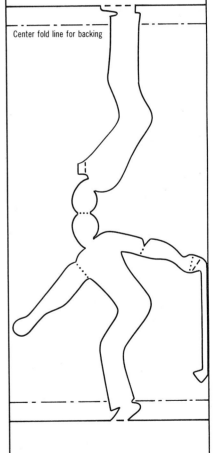

Center fold line for backing

⑬ **Sumo Wrestler,** *shown on page 4.*

Apply glue to head and hand.

Cutting line
.... Mountain fold (convex)
– – – – Valley fold (concave)

Center fold line for backing

㉟ **Question Mark,** *shown on page 10.*

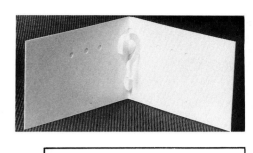

Cutting line
.... Mountain fold (convex)
– – – – Valley fold (concave)

㊽ **Bow Tie,** *shown on page 11.*

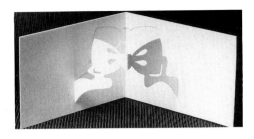

Cutting line

• • • • • • • Mountain fold
(convex)

— — — — Valley fold
(concave)

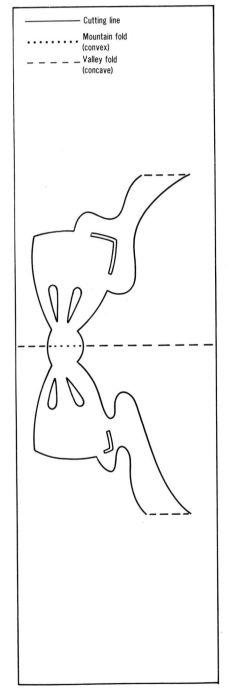

㉛ **Cupid's Arrow,** *shown on page 8.*

Point:
Cut Kent paper 2mm smaller than the colored backing paper. Glue red heart onto cut-out heart.

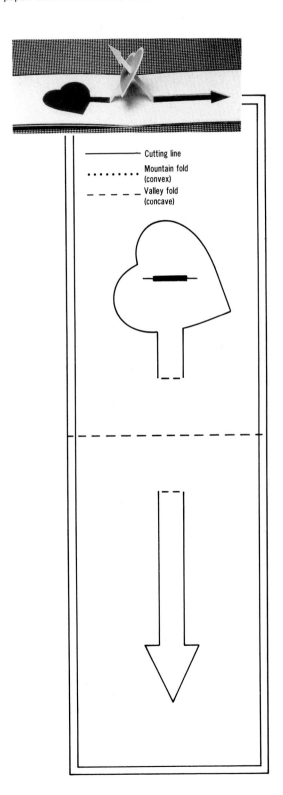

Cutting line

• • • • • • • Mountain fold
(convex)

— — — — Valley fold
(concave)

㊹ **Waves,** *shown on page 11.* ㉒ **Horse,** *shown on page 6.*

Point:
Use colored paper for backing.

———————	Cutting line
••••••••	Mountain fold (convex)
— — — —	Valley fold (concave)

——————— Cutting line

•••••••• Mountain fold (convex)

— — — — Valley fold (concave)

Apply glue to muzzle and tali.

Center fold line for backing

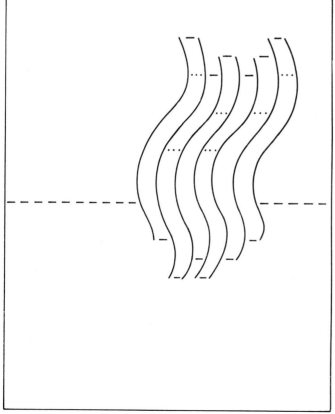

㊱ **Sunflower,** *shown on page 9.*

㉟ **Tulip,**

shown on page 9.

Cutting line

Mountain fold
(convex)

Valley fold
(concave)

ETUKO MOTOMURA
6-1-3-711 Ojima Koto Tokyo

Cutting line

Mountain fold
(convex)

Valley fold
(concavel)

Apply glue to tip of tulip and
bottom of stem.

Center fold line for backing

㉖ **Deer,** *shown on page 7.*

Apply glue to muzzle and tail.

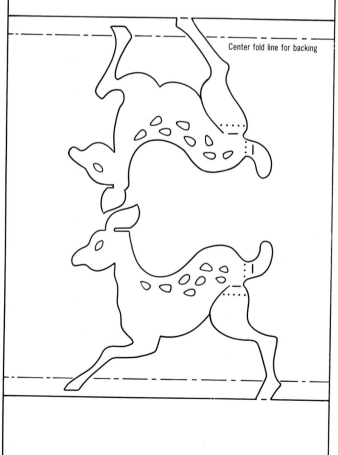

⑲ **Karate,**

shown on page 5.

Apply glue to head and tucked-in area.

—————— Cutting line

• • • • • • • • Mountain fold
(convex)

— — — — Valley fold
(concave)

—————— Cutting line

• • • • • • • • Mountain fold
(convex)

— — — — Valley fold
(concave)

Center fold line for backing

Center fold line for backing

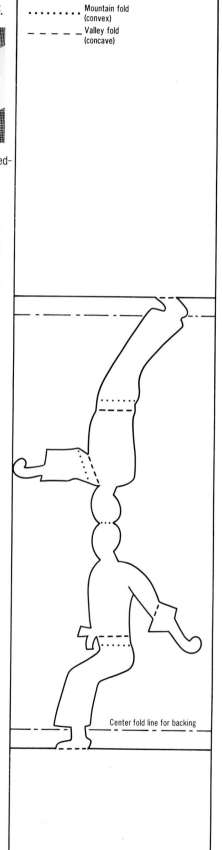

㊻ **Arch,** *shown on page 11.*

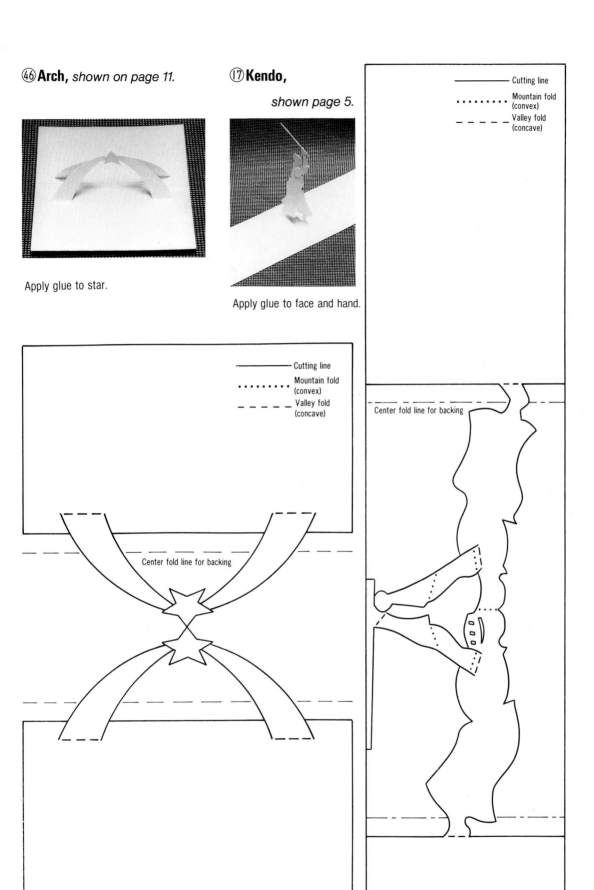

Apply glue to star.

⑰ **Kendo,**

shown page 5.

Apply glue to face and hand.

Cutting line
Mountain fold (convex)
Valley fold (concave)

Center fold line for backing

Cutting line
Mountain fold (convex)
Valley fold (concave)

Center fold line for backing

——————— Cutting line

•••••••• Mountain fold
(convex)

— — — — Valley fold
(concave)

Point:
Use colored paper for small heart.
Apply glue to head, tail, ribbon bow and
small heart.

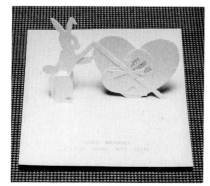

㊵ **Rising Sun,** *shown on page 10.*

——————— Cutting line
•••••••• Mountain fold
           (convex)
— — — — Valley fold
           (concave)

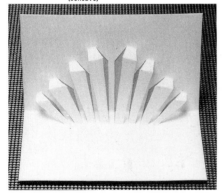

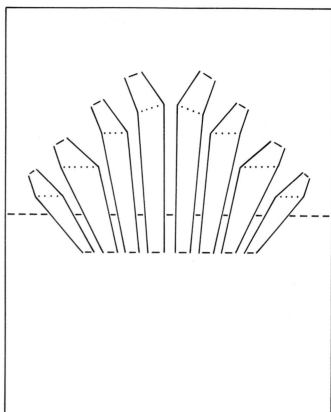

㊼ **City Night,** *shown on page 11.*

——————— Cutting line
•••••••• Mountain fold
           (convex)
— — — — Valley fold
           (concave)

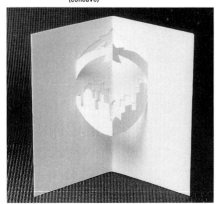

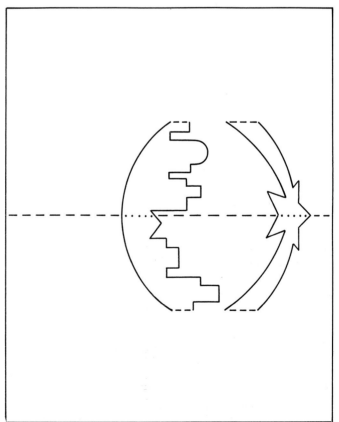

Apply glue to beak.

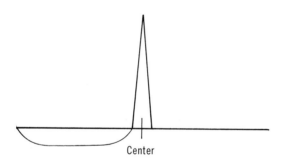

Center

8.5
cm

Center fold line for backing

——————— Cutting line

• • • • • • • • Mountain fold
(convex)

— — — — Valley fold
(concave)

㉞ **Iris,** *shown on page 9.*

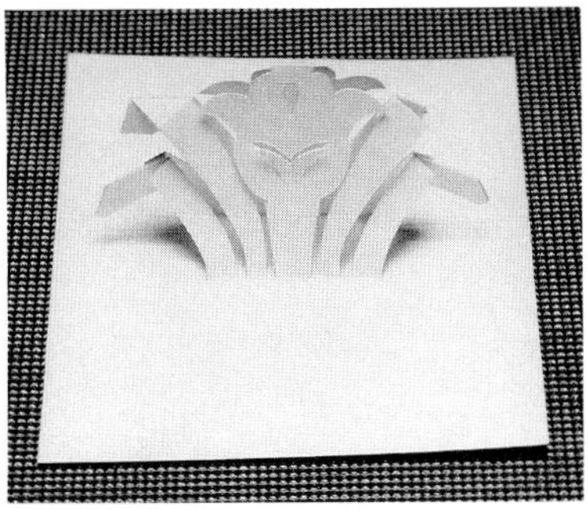

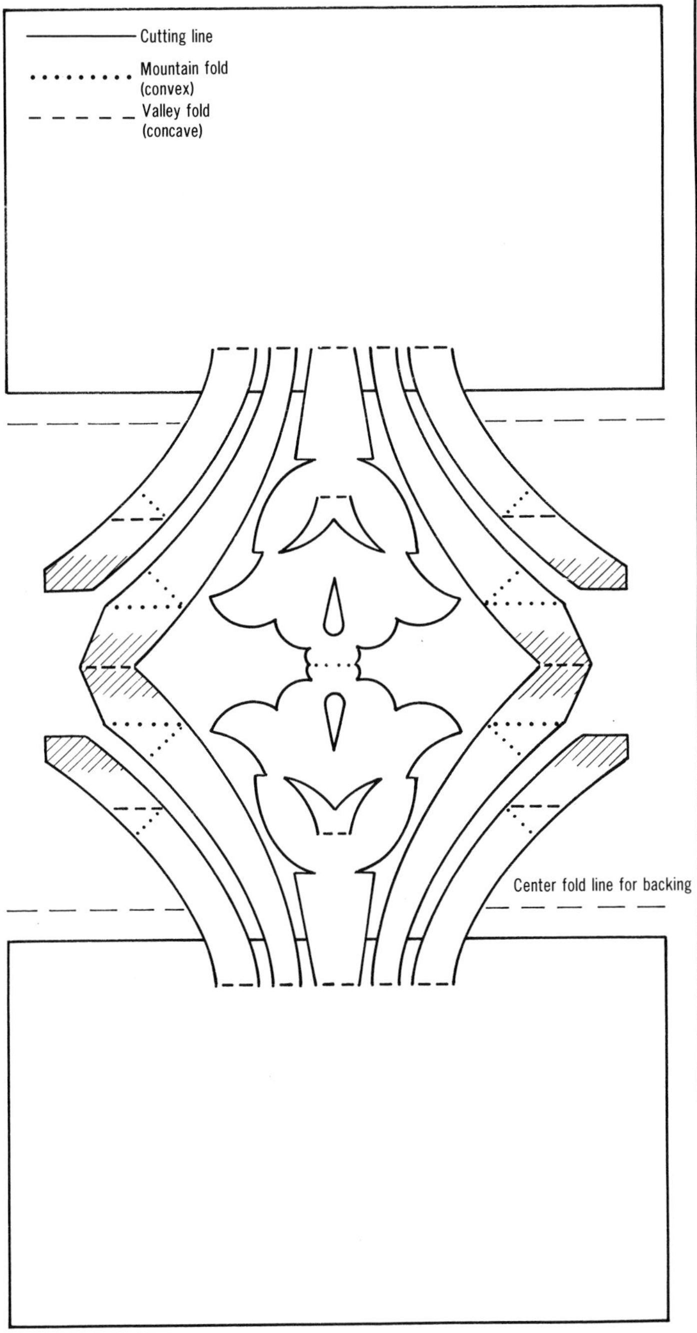

㊷ **Amoeba,** *shown on page 10.*

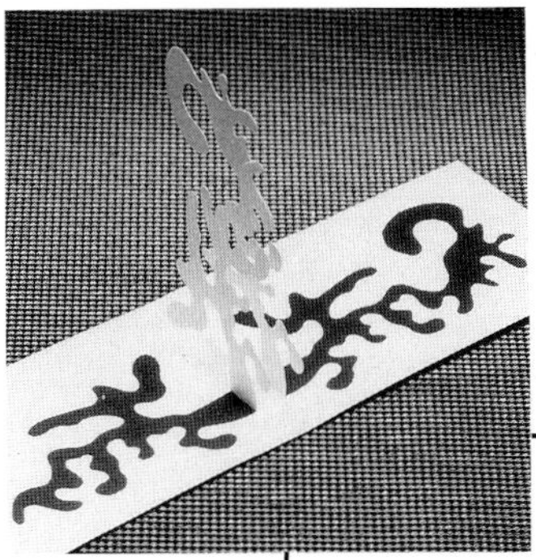

Apply glue to shaded area.

Apply glue to shorter tips.

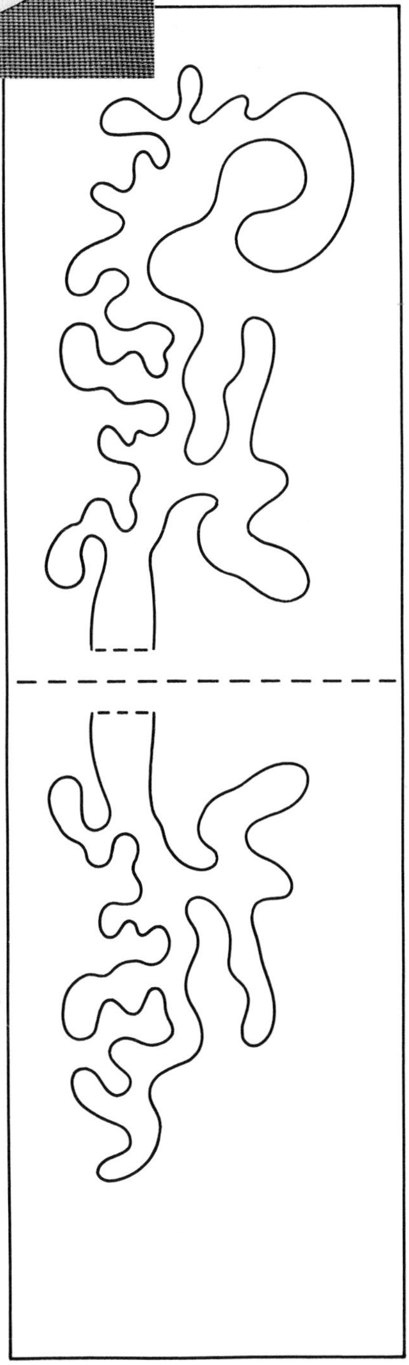

─────── Cutting line

• • • • • • • Mountain fold
(convex)

─ ─ ─ ─ Valley fold
(concave)

─────── Cutting line

• • • • • • • Mountain fold
(convex)

─ ─ ─ ─ Valley fold
(concave)

Center fold line for backing

61

㉟ **Skater,** *shown on page 5.*　　　　㊶ **Heart,** *shown on page 10.*

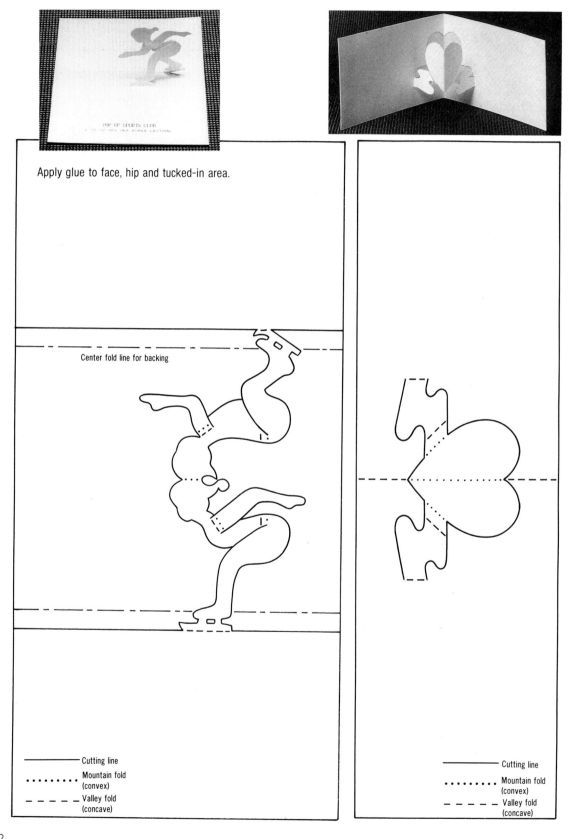

Apply glue to face, hip and tucked-in area.

Center fold line for backing

――――― Cutting line

•••••••• Mountain fold
(convex)

― ― ― ― Valley fold
(concave)

――――― Cutting line

•••••••• Mountain fold
(convex)

― ― ― ― Valley fold
(concave)

⑯ Swimmer, *shown on page 5.*

Apply glue to head and hip.

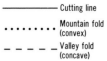
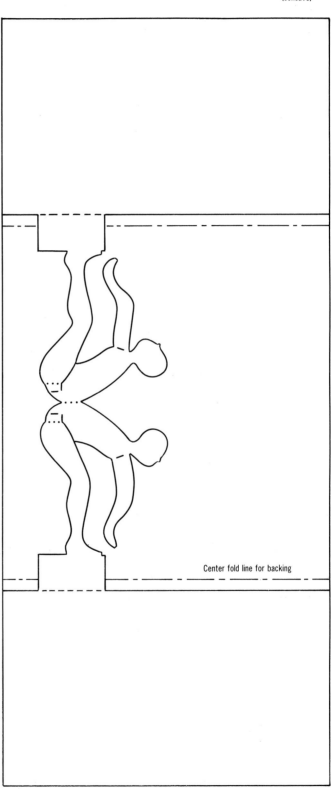

Center fold line for backing

㊷ **Name,** *shown on page 13.*

Point:
Use colored paper for backing.

——— Cutting line
• • • • • • • • • Mountain fold (convex)
— — — — — Valley fold (concave)

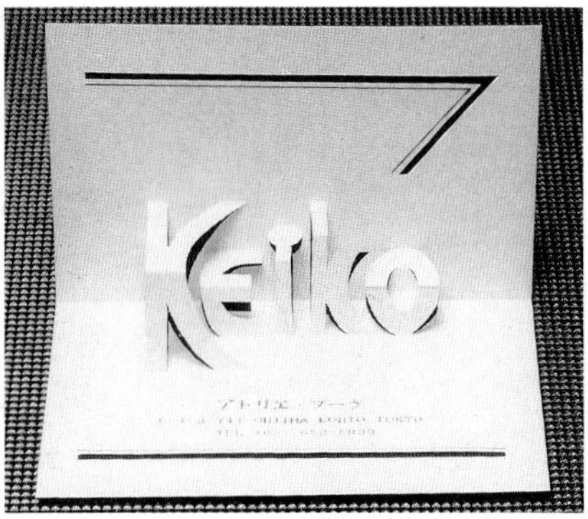

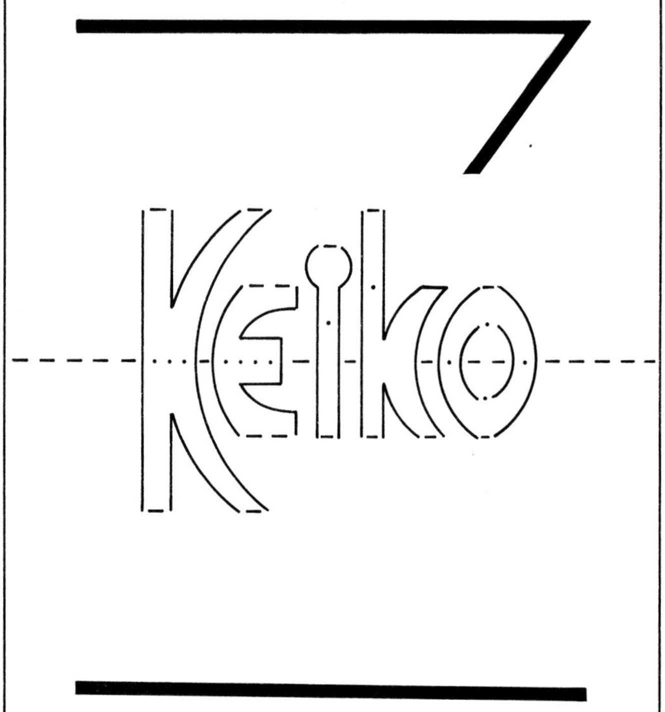

● Cut out the black-colored area.

㊹ **Name,** *shown on page 13.*

——— Cutting line
• • • • • • • • • Mountain fold (convex)
— — — — — Valley fold (concave)

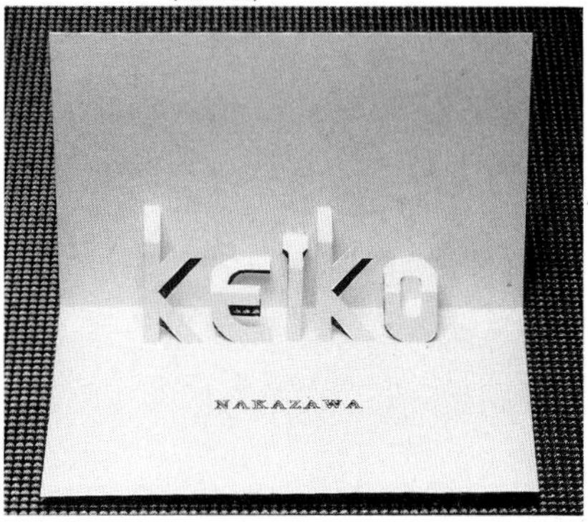

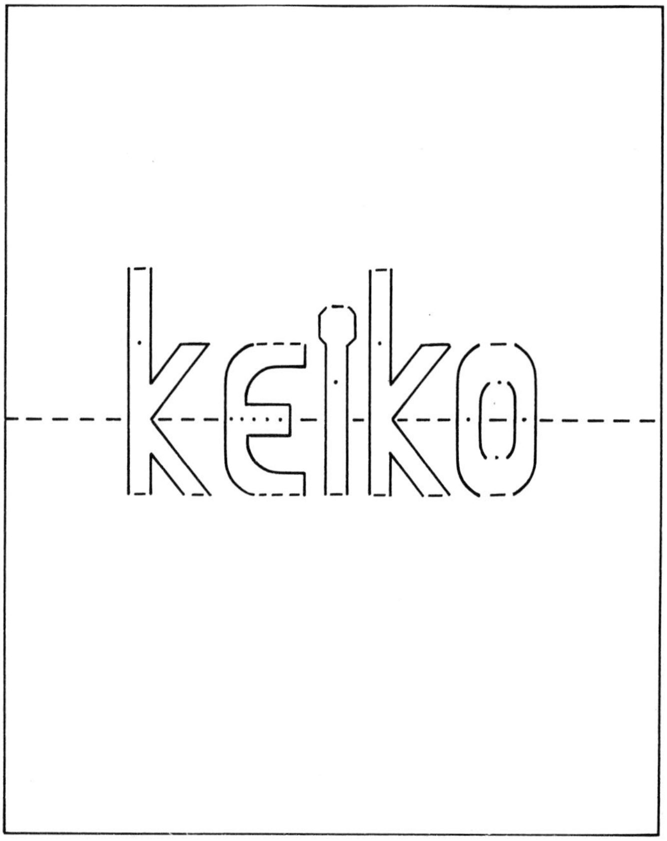

㉕ **Antelope,** *shown on page 7.*

Apply glue to tail and muzzle.

● Mountain-fold and Valley-fold lines are reversed in this diagram so that they cannot be seen on front. When you fold along the lines, the object will pop up on the reverse side.

———————— Cutting line

– – – – – Valley fold ↿ (concave)

• • • • • • • Mountain fold (convex)

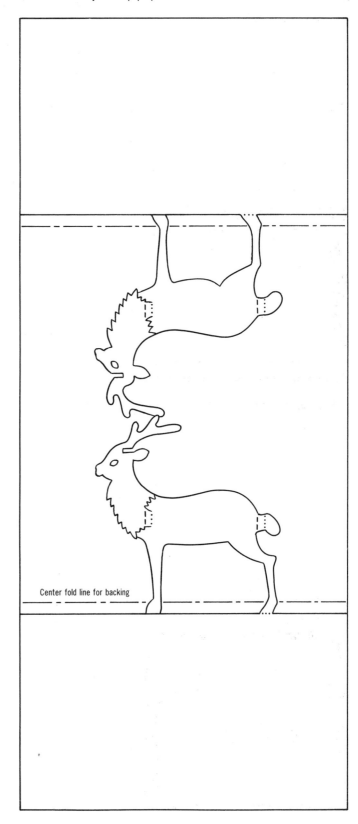

Center fold line for backing

⑨**Dove,** *shown on page 3.*

—————— Cutting line
— — — — — Valley fold (concave)
• • • • • • • Mountain fold (convex)

● Mountain-fold and Valley-fold lines are reversed in this diagram so that they cannot be seen on front. When you fold along the lines, the object will pop up on the reverse side.

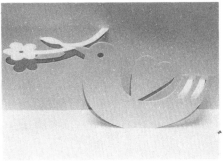

㉜**Angels,** *shown on page 8.*

—————— Cutting line
— — — — — Valley fold (concave)
• • • • • • • Mountain fold (convex)

Point:
Cut out open heart from red Kent paper and place on the hand.

● Mountain-fold and Valley-fold lines are reversed in this diagram so that they cannot be seen on front. When you fold along the lines, the object will pop up on the reverse side.

ETUKO MOTOMURA
6-1-3-711 OJIMA KOTO
TOKYO

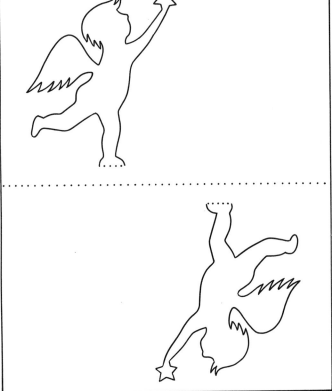

㊳ Lily of the Valley,

shown on page 9.

———————— Cutting line

– – – – – Valley fold (concave)

•••••••• Mountain fold (convex)

● Mountain-fold and Valley-fold lines are reversed in this diagram so that they cannot be seen on front. When you fold along the lines, the odject will pop up on the reverse side.

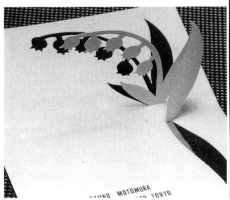

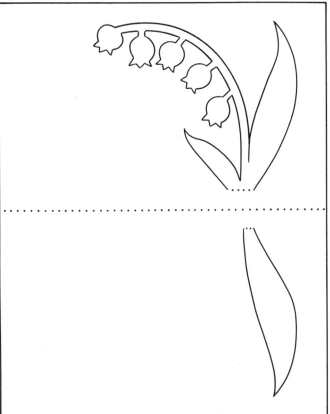

㊲ Kitten and Flower,

shown on page 9.

———————— Cutting line

– – – – – Valley fold (concave)

•••••••• Mountain fold (convex)

● Mountain-fold and Valley-fold lines are reversed in this diagram so that they cannot be seen on front. When you fold along the lines, the object will pop up on the reverse side.

⑧**Swan,** *shown on page 3.*

● Mountain-fold and Valley-fold lines are reversed in this diagram so that they cannot be seen on front. When you fold along the lines, the object will pop up on the reverse side.

Apply glue to beak and tail.

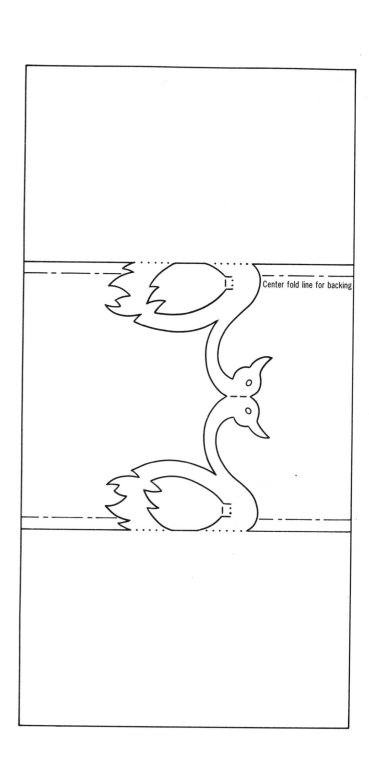

Center fold line for backing

——————— Cutting line
– – – – – Valley fold (concave)
• • • • • • • Mountain fold (convex)

④ **Duckling,** *shown on page 2.*

● Mountain-fold and Valley-fold lines are reversed in this diagram so that they cannot be seen on front. When you fold along the lines, the object will pop up on the reverse side.

Apply glue to beak and tail.

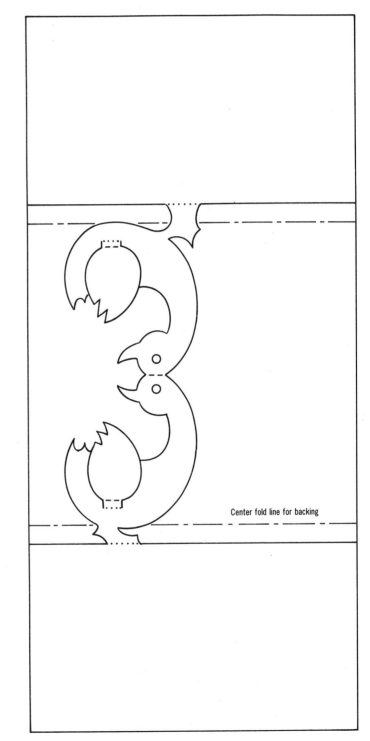

Center fold line for backing

———————— Cutting line

— — — — — Valley fold (concave)

• • • • • • • • Mountain fold (convex)

㉑**Pitcher,** *shown on page 5.*

● Mountain-fold and Valley-fold lines are reversed in this diagram so that they cannot be seen on front. When you fold along the lines, the object will pop up on the reverse side.

Apply glue to face.

Center fold line for backing

——————— Cutting line
— — — — — Valley fold (concave)
•••••••• Mountain fold (convex)

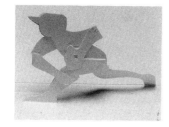

● Mountain-fold and Valley-fold lines are reversed in this diagram so that they cannot be seen on front. When you fold along the lines, the object will pop up on the reverse side.

Apply glue to head and hand.

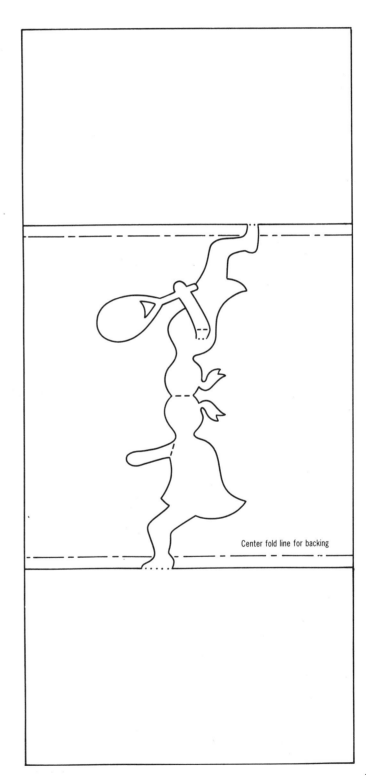

Center fold line for backing

――――――― Cutting line

― ― ― ― ― Valley fold (concave)

• • • • • • • • Mountain fold (convex)